Dr. Seuss's ABC

Random House 🏠 New York

BIG A
little   a

What begins with A?

Aunt Annie's alligator .

. . . . . A . . a . . A

BIG B

little   b

What begins with B?

Barber
baby
bubbles
and a
bumblebee.

BIG C

little c

What begins with C?

Camel on the ceiling
C . . . . c C

BIG D

little   d

David Donald Doo
dreamed
a dozen doughnuts
and
a duck-dog, too.

ABCDE . . e . . e

ear

egg

elephant

e

e

E

BIG F

little   f

F . . f . . F

Four fluffy feathers
on a
Fiffer-feffer-feff.

17

ABCD
EFG

Goat
girl
googoo goggles
G . . . g . . . G

19

BIG H

little   h

Hungry horse.
Hay.

Hen in a hat.
Hooray!
Hooray!

BIG I

little   i

i . . . . i i

Icabod
is
itchy.

So am I.

BIG J

little   j

What begins with j?

Jerry Jordan's
jelly jar
and jam
begin that way.

BIG K

little   k

Kitten. Kangaroo.

Kick a kettle.
Kite
and a
king's kerchoo.

BIG L

little   l

Little Lola Lopp.
Left leg.
Lazy lion
licks a lollipop.

BIG M

little   m

Many mumbling mice
are making
midnight music
in the moonlight . . .

mighty nice

31

BIG N

little   n

What begins with those?

Nine new neckties
and a nightshirt
and a nose.

O is very useful.
You use it when you say:
"Oscar's only ostrich
oiled
an orange owl today."

35

ABCD EFG HIJK LMNO.

...**P**

Painting pink pajamas.
Policeman in a pail.

Peter Pepper's puppy.
And now
Papa's in the pail.

BIG Q

little   q

What begins with Q?

The quick
Queen of Quincy
and her
quacking quacker-oo.

QUACK
QUACK

41

BIG R
little   r

Rosy Robin Ross.

Rosy's going riding
on her
red rhinoceros.

BIG S

little   s

Silly Sammy Slick
sipped six sodas
and got
sick sick sick.

T . . . . T
t . . . . t

What begins with T?

Ten tired turtles
on a tuttle-tuttle tree.

BIG U

little   u

What begins with U?

Uncle Ubb's umbrella
and his
underwear, too.

BIG V

little   v

Vera Violet Vinn
is
very
very
very awful
on her violin.

W . . w . . W

Willy Waterloo
washes Warren Wiggins
who is
washing Waldo Woo.

X is very useful
if your name is
Nixie Knox.
It also
comes in handy
spelling ax
and extra fox.

NIXIE KNOX

BIG Y

little y

A yawning yellow yak.
Young Yolanda Yorgenson
is yelling on his back.

58

QRS
TUV...

W..X
Y.. and.....

BIG Z

little z

What begins with Z?

I do.
I am a
Zizzer-Zazzer-Zuzz
as you can
plainly see.